SUZY KLINE

HERBIE JONES

AND THE
Second Grade Slippers

ILLUSTRATED BY **SAMI SWEETEN**

G. P. PUTNAM'S SONS

Special appreciation for:

Daria Plummer, Connecticut Teacher of the Year, and her fourth-grade class at Wapping Elementary in South Windsor, who are shoeless wonders!

Barbara Pettersen and her second-graders at Frank G. Lindsey Elementary School in Montrose, New York, who love to learn in their slippers each day.

And Kreschell Morris and her third-graders at Eastbury Elementary School in Glastonbury, Connecticut, who wrote delightful "Don't laugh at me" stories!

Thank you for inspiring this story!

—Suzy Kline

G. P. PUTNAM'S SONS
A division of Penguin Young Readers Group
Published by The Penguin Group
Penguin Group (USA) Inc., 375 Hudson Street, New York, NY 10014, U.S.A.
Penguin Group (Canada), 90 Eglinton Avenue East, Toronto, Ontario, Canada M4P 2Y3
(a division of Pearson Penguin Canada Inc.).
Penguin Books Ltd, 80 Strand, London WC2R 0RL, England.
Penguin Ireland, 25 St. Stephen's Green, Dublin 2, Ireland (a division of Penguin Books Ltd.).
Penguin Group (Australia), 250 Camberwell Road,
Camberwell, Victoria 3124, Australia (a division of Pearson Australia Group Pty Ltd).
Penguin Books India Pvt Ltd, 11 Community Centre, Panchsheel Park, New Delhi - 110 017, India.
Penguin Group (NZ), Cnr Airborne and Rosedale Roads,
Albany, Auckland 1310, New Zealand (a division of Pearson New Zealand Ltd).
Penguin Books (South Africa) (Pty) Ltd, 24 Sturdee Avenue, Rosebank,
Johannesburg 2196, South Africa.
Penguin Books Ltd, Registered Offices: 80 Strand, London WC2R 0RL, England.

Published simultaneously in Canada. Printed in the United States of America.
Design by Cecilia Yung and Marikka Tamura. Text set in 14-point Stone Informal.

Library of Congress Cataloging-in-Publication Data
Kline, Suzy. Herbie Jones and the second grade slippers / Suzy Kline ;
illustrated by Sami Sweeten. p. cm.
Summary: Herbie, Ray, and their second-grade classmates learn more about treating
each other with respect. [1. Self-esteem—Fiction. 2. Interpersonal relations—Fiction.
3. Schools—Fiction.] I. Sweeten, Sami, ill. II. Title.
PZ7.K6797Hig 2006 [Fic]—dc22 2005003537
ISBN 0-399-23132-3
1 3 5 7 9 10 8 6 4 2
First Impression

Contents

Chapter One: Sailor Hats and Guppies 1

Chapter Two: The Big Announcement 7

Chapter Three: Don't Laugh! 12

Chapter Four: The Secret Phone Call 25

Chapter Five: The Slipper Problem 33

Chapter Six: Second Grade Slippers 40

Chapter Seven: Second Grade Bathrobes? 46

Chapter One
Sailor Hats and Guppies

Herbie and Raymond walked into their classroom. Herbie took his sailor hat off a hook and put it on his head. Ray did the same.

"I like sailing through second grade," Herbie said. "Mr. S makes school fun."

"He does," Ray replied. Then he took out a notebook and pen from his backpack.

"What's your phone number, Herbie?"

"525-3942." Herbie was glad Raymond had just moved into his neighborhood from Minnesota. "Now you give me yours, Ray."

While the boys were exchanging numbers, Annabelle Louisa Hodgekiss came up behind them.

"Excuse me," she said. "I need to get my sailor hat."

Herbie noticed Annabelle's still looked brand-new. It didn't have any dirty finger smudges on it like his and Ray's.

Before the morning bell rang, some kids gathered around the ten-gallon tank in the science corner. The silvery green guppies were swimming around.

"There are twelve," Margie counted.

"Four more than Friday," Herbie added.

"See the four biggest ones?" Annabelle asked. "They're females."

"I'm gl-glad Mr. S br-brought them in," Sarah Sitwellington said.

Annabelle giggled. Then she said, "Guppies come from Venezuela and

Trinidad. They help control mosquitoes by feeding on their larvae."

Ray made a face. He had no idea what *larvae* meant. Annabelle was a big know-it-all, he thought.

"I l-l-love g-guppies," Sarah replied.

When Annabelle giggled again, Sarah went back to her seat and put her head down on her desk.

Margie shook her head. "You hurt her feelings, Annabelle! You should never laugh at someone who stutters."

Annabelle shrugged.

Mr. Schnellenberger looked over. He had heard the entire conversation.

Annabelle! Herbie thought. He felt like tossing her overboard!

Chapter Two
The Big Announcement

After the bell rang and the children sat down, Mr. S made a big announcement.

"Boys and girls, I want you to feel comfortable in our classroom. So . . . we're going to take our shoes off."

Ray's eyes bulged.

"We'll be helping the custodian too,"

the teacher explained, "by not tracking in dirt on the new carpet."

Herbie put two thumbs in the air. He loved the idea.

"Go ahead and take off your shoes now. Just make sure they stay under your own desk. Tomorrow, you can start bringing in your slippers. I'll send home a notice about it to your parents today."

Everyone cheered and clapped except Raymond.

Annabelle was beaming. "I'll have to decide which pair to bring."

Herbie wrinkled his forehead. He wondered how someone could have more than one pair of slippers. Then he remembered his sister, Olivia, had just gotten a new pair. So she kind of had two if you counted the old pair in the laundry room.

Lots of kids were giggling as they took off their shoes.

Not Sarah Sitwellington.

Her head was still down on her desk. Mr. S went over and talked with Sarah.

A few minutes later he returned to the front of the room. "We're going to do something else so everyone can feel more comfortable."

"Take off our socks?" Ray blurted out.

Mr. S put his hand up like a stop sign. "No, no! You must leave your socks on. What we're going to do is write 'Don't laugh at me' stories."

Sarah sat up and listened.

Herbie and Ray exchanged a look.

"For example," Mr. S said, "I don't want anyone laughing at my big ears. When I was a second-grader, some kids called me Dumbo. You know that elephant, the one with the enormous ears."

Some kids nodded.

"It didn't make me feel very good."

More kids shook their heads.

"Now it's your turn to tell a 'Don't laugh at me' story," Mr. S said.

Chapter Three
Don't Laugh!

Herbie got started right away:

I don't spel well, but I lick to rite. It's no fun to have someone laff at your storey becuse the werds are speld rong. I don't lick it. If you no how to spell a werd, you can tell me. Jess don't laff.

When Herbie looked up, lots of kids were still writing.

Ten minutes later, Mr. S passed around his plastic microphone. "I love the way you read your work on the microphone. We can hear every word. This time, though, I want you to do something extra. When the person is finished reading, clap  your index fingers if you won't laugh. It's kind of like a promise you'll try to keep."

Herbie practiced clapping his fingers. It hardly made a noise, but it was fun.

"Who wants to go first?" Mr. S asked.

Everyone looked at Annabelle. Her hand was not up. That's strange, Herbie thought.

"I'm ready," Ray said.

"All right!" Mr. S replied.

Ray put the mouthpiece a little away

from his mouth and began: "Don't laugh at me when I read a word wrong. It stinks. But guess what? I can read three enormous words. Vikings, Minnesota, and cheeseburgers."

When everyone laughed, Ray looked confused.

"That laugh was not a mean one, Ray," Mr. S explained. "You write funny endings. We enjoyed your story. See? Look around."

Ray did. Everyone was clapping their index fingers.

"The class says they won't laugh, Ray, if you read a word wrong," Mr. S said.

Sarah went next. "I stutter. I don't like it when I can't get the words out. I don't stutter when I read, or sing. I see a speech therapist. She's nice and she helps me. Please don't laugh at me when I stutter, it makes me sad."

As soon as she finished, Sarah looked up. Every single person was clapping their index fingers. Even Annabelle.

Sarah beamed. The class promised.

Then Margie shared her story. "I can't read well. I make a lot of mistakes."

Raymond and Margie exchanged a smile.

"Sometimes," she continued, "someone laughs at me when I read a word wrong, like 'Fred' for 'friend,' and 'poop' for 'pop.'"

Most of the children covered their mouths. They tried hard not to laugh. But there was giggling.

"You bring up an interesting point, Margie," Mr. S said. "There are some words that make us laugh. We can't help it. You just said 'poop.' That makes us laugh. So does 'underwear.' But that kind of laughing is not mean."

Margie nodded. "I know what you're saying, Mr. S. I always giggle when Mom says we're going to order the poo poo platter."

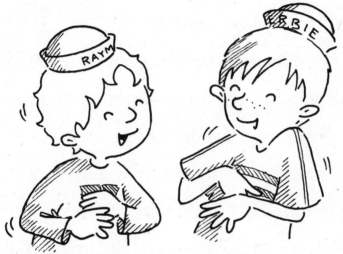

Herbie and Ray cracked up.

Mr. S chuckled too. "That's a great example, Margie."

When everyone clapped their fingers, Margie pumped her hand in the air.

"Now . . . let's see," the teacher said, "who else wants to share their 'Don't laugh at me' story?"

John did. He asked the class not to laugh at his asthma problem.

Phillip asked the class not to laugh when he got a booger. He said just tell him about it. He carried handkerchiefs.

Annabelle was last. She slowly took the microphone. Herbie was curious about what she'd say. Annabelle was the best speller and reader and she didn't have big ears or boogers.

Annabelle cleared her throat. "I think I wrote something different."

"Good," Mr. S replied. "I like variety."

Annabelle held up her paper. Herbie noticed her sentences were written neatly. "I know a lot of facts. Even about guppies. Sometimes I don't share them because people think I'm showing off. Please don't laugh at me because I'm smart."

Mr. S looked at his students. They were clapping their fingers. "The class says they won't laugh, Annabelle!"

Annabelle clasped her hands together like she had just won a soccer game.

"W-what are the extra g-guppy facts?" Sarah asked. "I'd l-l-like to kn-know."

Annabelle gave Sarah a warm smile. "Well, we have fancy guppies at home in our aquarium."

"You do?" Ray said.

Annabelle nodded. "They are wild guppies of Florida. Their water has to stay between 75 and 85 degrees. I check the floating thermometer in our tank every day. They have a reddish brown body and their tails have black dots. I can bring a picture of them to class."

"Cool," Herbie replied.

"Bravo, class," Mr. S said. "I'm putting your great stories up on our bulletin board. I'm hoping they will remind us all to be kind to one another."

Herbie nodded.

He decided he wouldn't toss Annabelle off their second-grade ship. At least not right now.

• • •

At the end of the day, Mr. S handed out the notices. "Don't forget to bring in your slippers tomorrow."

Ray quickly crumpled his up and stuffed it into his desk. He wasn't bringing his notice home.

Chapter Four
The Secret Phone Call

Ray didn't feeling like kicking a can with Herbie on their way home from school.

Olivia, who always walked with the boys, noticed Ray's mood. "What's the matter?" she asked.

"Nothing," Ray moaned.

No one said much the rest of the way.

When they got to Ray's house, they could see his puppy, Shadow, pawing at the screen door. He was excited to see Ray coming up the sidewalk.

Ray's shoulders slumped as he walked up the porch. His puppy's welcome did not cheer him up.

Olivia just shrugged.

As soon as they stepped into the house, the phone rang. Mrs. Jones was out shopping. Mr. Jones was doing the crossword in the newspaper and having coffee. He had a night job and got up just before Herbie and Olivia got home from school.

"Hi, kids!" he called from the kitchen. "How was your day?"

Olivia and Herbie ran to the phone before they answered their dad. Olivia got there first. "Hello?" she said in a sweet voice.

"Just a minute," she groaned. "It's for you."

"Me?" Herbie wondered who it was. He didn't get too many calls. "Is it Grandpa?"

"No."

Olivia handed him the phone.

"Hello?" Herbie said.

"Hi, Herbie."

"Ray! I didn't think you'd call so soon."

"It's an emergency, Herbie. This call has to be private."

Herbie looked around.

Private?

In this house?

Herbie pulled on the phone cord. It was curly, but if you stretched it out, you could take it to other places.

Herbie looked around.

Yes!

The smallest room in the house. The pantry!

Herbie took the phone into the little closet, shut the door, and sat down on a sack of potatoes.

"Okay, Ray," he whispered. "I'm in the pantry with the canned beans. What's up?"

"This is so secret, I think we should make up spy names like that famous guy Double-0-7."

"Cool, Ray! What's your name?"

"It should be at least a three-digit number. How about . . . 9-9-2? Over."

"Over?" Herbie said. "What do you mean 'over'?"

"That's what spies say when it's the other guy's turn to talk," Ray said.

"Oh. Okay. So I'll be . . ." Herbie paused. "Double-0-3-0. Over."

"Roger, Double-0-3-0."

"Roger?" Herbie interrupted. "Roger who?"

"No, Herbie. 'Roger' means 'I got it.' My dad teaches me all this stuff."

"Okey-dokey. Now I get it," Herbie replied.

"Okay. This is 9-9-2," Ray said. "I have a problem. Over."

"Roger," Herbie said. "This is Double-0-3-0. What's wrong? Over." Herbie liked using their new code language.

"What I'm going to tell you is top secret, Double-0-3-0."

"Roger, 9-9-2."

"I don't have any slippers. I can't ask my dad to buy me a pair either. I heard him

talking to Mom yesterday about how expensive moving was. He said we couldn't afford one more thing. Over."

"Roger. I think I have a solution, 9-9-2," Herbie said.

"You do, Double-0-3-0?"

"We have an extra pair at my house. I'll give you one tomorrow, 9-9-2. Over."

"Roger. Man, that's super! Thank you. See you on the corner tomorrow, Double-0-3-0. Over and out."

"Roger. See you tomorrow, 9-9-2. Over and out."

When Herbie hung up, he made a long sigh. He had left out one important detail.

That extra pair was his sister's.

Chapter Five
The Slipper Problem

As soon as Herbie hung up the phone, Olivia grabbed it. "My turn, finally!" Then she took it into the dining room and closed the door.

Herbie thought the pantry was a better place for private talks. But he knew Olivia would never sit on a bag of potatoes or onions.

"What's up, Herb?" his dad asked. He noticed his son's long face.

Herbie got an oatmeal cookie and some milk and joined his dad at the table.

Mr. Jones put his newspaper down.

"I've got an enormous problem, Dad."

Herbie told him all about it.

"Well, why don't you get those slippers and let's see how bad things are."

Herbie ran to the laundry room. There in the corner was a box of old stuff. On top were Olivia's purple mules with tiny flowers along the edges.

When Herbie brought them into the kitchen, Mr. Jones cracked up.

"You know, Dad," Herbie said, "you shouldn't laugh at people. I learned that in school today."

"I agree, son, but I'm not laughing at a person. I'm laughing at those slippers. No one's wearing them."

"Ray might."

Mr. Jones put his coffee down. "O-kay," he said slowly. He tried to be positive. "They don't look that worn."

"They're easy to slip on and off," Herbie added. "They're backless."

"But they do look like . . ."

"Girls' slippers," Herbie groaned.

"Well, you know," his father said. "Times are changing. Things are more unisex right now."

"*Unisex*? What's that?"

Mr. Jones took a sip of his coffee. "It means both boys and girls can use it or wear it. We have a unisex bathroom at my factory. Men and women both use it."

Herbie lowered his eyebrows, and his voice. "No kidding?"

"No kidding."

"Hmmm . . . ," Herbie said, "purple is Ray's favorite color."

"That's a plus," Mr. Jones replied. It was quiet for a moment.

"I wouldn't want to wear those two slippers at school," Herbie confessed.

"Me neither," his dad agreed.

Suddenly, Herbie got an idea. It all came from that word he just said, *two*!

"I got it, Dad! I know what to do!" Then Herbie grabbed the slippers and raced out of the kitchen.

"I'm proud of you, son!" Mr. Jones yelled. "You figured out your own solution!" Then he wondered what in the world it was.

Chapter Six
Second Grade Slippers

The next morning Herbie put two bags in his backpack—one with his slippers and one with Ray's.

Raymond was waiting for Herbie and his sister on the corner. "Did you bring them?" he asked right away.

Herbie gave his buddy the A-OK sign.

"Got 'em right here, 9-9-2," Herbie replied, patting his backpack.

"Roger, Double-0-3-0." Ray knew they were not alone.

"What are you guys talking about?" Olivia asked.

Ray flashed a toothy smile. "Sorry, it's top secret. We can't tell."

Olivia rolled her eyes.

When the boys got to their classroom, Herbie and Ray grabbed their sailor hats, then made a beeline to the cloakroom.

"Okay, Ray. I have to tell you something."

"Yeah?"

"That extra pair of slippers I had for you . . ."

"Yeah?"

"Well, I left out one major detail."

"What detail?" Ray asked.

Herbie opened up his backpack and handed him a brown bag.

Ray took it, and reached inside. "Whoa. This has flowers on it. It's a girls' slipper!"

"Yup."

Then Ray pulled out a second slipper with a dog's head. "How cool is that!" he exclaimed.

Herbie nodded.
"I've got the
same pair,
buddy. I knew
I couldn't wear
two flowered slippers,
but I figured we could each wear one and tough it out."

Ray held up one thumb.

Herbie held up one thumb.

Then the boys put their slippers on, took a deep breath, and walked into the classroom.

Everyone looked over at Herbie and Ray, then stared down at their feet.

No one said a word.

Mr. S smiled. "They look real comfortable!" he said. "And unique."

"They're unisex," Herbie explained.

No one laughed.

Annabelle ran to the dictionary.

Herbie and Ray slapped each other five.
They did it!

And when Herbie looked at the bulletin
board with their great stories, he knew why.

His class remembered their promise.

Chapter Seven

Second Grade Bathrobes?

Herbie couldn't wait to call his grandpa. He knew his number by heart.

"Collect call for Grandpa Jones from Herbie Jones," Herbie said into the phone.

"One moment, please," the operator replied.

While he waited, Herbie counted the holes in the receiver. There were seven.

"Go ahead, please," the operator said.

"Howdy, howdy, howdy!" Grandpa sang out.

"Grandpa! My class gets to wear slippers in second grade!"

"Holy moly!" Grandpa said. "Slippers in school! Landsakes! What next?"

"Neato, huh?" Herbie answered. "And guess what?"

"You get to wear bathrobes too?"

"No, Grandpa!"

"Pajamas?"

"NO!" Herbie loved their guessing games.

"Are you wearing lampshades on your head?" Grandpa asked.

"NO! NO! I'll tell you what. . . . My friend Ray and me—you remember him, right?"

"Sure," Grandpa said. "He's the guy who likes to write about food."

"Yup," Herbie replied. "Ray and me have the exact same pair of slippers."

"The exact same pair?"

"Actually, one's a dog slipper, and the other is a flowered mule."

"A flowered mule? I didn't know don-keys had flowers on them."

"GRANDPA . . . a mule is a backless slipper. It's the kind Olivia wears."

The phone went quiet for a moment.

"You're wearing one girls' slipper?" Grandpa asked.

"Yup. Ray is too. He didn't have a pair, so it was the best I could do. We're sharing Olivia's old pair."

"Herbie?"

"Yes, Grandpa."

"I wish I was in second grade again. You know why?"

"No. Why?" Herbie asked.

"Because I could have you for a buddy every day in school. You're the best, Herbie."

"You mean it?"

"It's rootin-tootin' true," Grand-pa said.

"I love you, Grandpa."

"I love you, Herbie. Toodle-loo, buga-boo."

"Toodle-loo to you too," Herbie replied.

Second Grade Snapshots

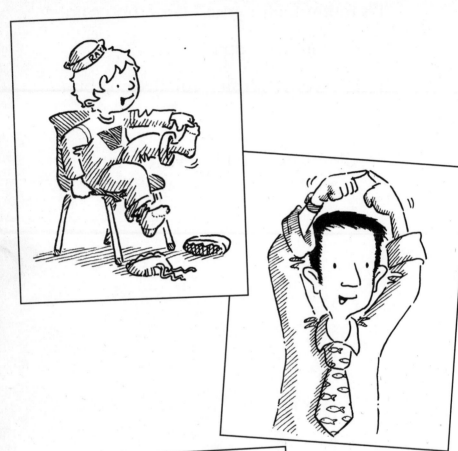

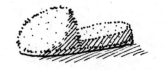